Pandemics

CULTURE SHIFT
THEN AND NOW

Abdo & Daughters
MIDDLE GRADE NONFICTION
An imprint of Abdo Publishing
abdobooks.com

Elsie Olson

Design: Kelly Doudna, Mighty Media, Inc.

Production: Mighty Media, Inc.

Editor: Jessica Rusick

Cover Photographs: MICHAEL REYNOLDS/EPA-EFE/Shutterstock Images (right); National Archives and Records Administration

Interior Photographs: 500/iStockphoto, p. 36; AP Images, p. 40; arnau pascual/Wikimedia Commons, p. 14; The Crowley Company/Library of Congress, pp. 10–11; Fadel Dawood/AP Images, p. 8; George Rinhart/Getty Images, p. 20; H.F. Schoof/CDC, p. 29 (top); Heritage Images/Getty Images, p. 24; Library of Congress, p. 12; MICHAEL REYNOLDS/EPA-EFE/Shutterstock Images, p. 1 (right); MONUSCO Photos/Flickr, p. 29; National Archives and Records Administration, pp. 1, 6 (both), 18, 19, 21, 22, 28; NIAID/Flickr, p. 30; nycshooter/iStockphoto, pp. 4–5; Phil Roeder/Flickr, pp. 38, 39 (top); Shutterstock Images, pp. 7, 9, 13, 26–27, 34, 35, 39, 41, 42, 44; State Library of Queensland, p. 15; US Naval History and Heritage Command, pp. 16–17, 45; USEMBKL/Flickr, p. 31; wanderluster/iStockphoto, pp. 32–33; Wikimedia Commons, p. 25

Design Elements: Shutterstock Images

LIBRARY OF CONGRESS CONTROL NUMBER: 2020949736

PUBLISHER'S CATALOGING-IN-PUBLICATION DATA

Names: Olson, Elsie, author

Title: Culture shift: then and now / by Elsie Olson

Other title: then and now

Description: Minneapolis, Minnesota : Abdo Publishing, 2022 | Series: Pandemics | Includes online resources and index

Identifiers: ISBN 9781532195587 (lib. bdg.) | ISBN 9781098216313 (ebook)

Subjects: LCSH: Social change--Juvenile literature. | Social evolution--Juvenile literature. | Culture and interpersonal relations--Juvenile literature. | Epidemics--History--Juvenile literature. | Diseases and history--Juvenile literature. | Medical archaeology--Juvenile literature

Classification: DDC 614.5--dc23

TABLE OF CONTENTS

Disease and Culture 5

Influenza Attacks 11

Pandemic Culture 17

A Social Shift 27

COVID Culture 33

Timeline 44

Glossary 46

Online Resources 47

Index 48

During the COVID-19 pandemic, some parks painted circles on the ground to encourage social distancing.

Chapter 1

DISEASE AND CULTURE

Throughout human history, culture has been shaped by historical events. Wars, natural disasters, and pandemics can all transform a society's customs, beliefs, and social conventions. Such events can change how people behave, socialize, and make art.

In 2020, a new pandemic changed the lives of many people around the world. A pandemic is the worldwide spread of a disease. During a pandemic, new infections occur at the same time in many different places. The 2020 pandemic was caused by a novel coronavirus called SARS-CoV-2. This virus caused a new disease called coronavirus disease 2019, or COVID-19 for short.

COVID-19 was first detected in Wuhan, China, in late 2019. By March 2020, the disease had spread to more than 100 countries. By the end of 2020, the disease had infected more than 83 million people worldwide, killing more than 1.8 million. The COVID-19 pandemic also changed daily life for billions of people around the world.

1918 Pandemic

COVID-19 was the worst pandemic in generations. But it wasn't the first pandemic to affect the world. In 1918, the world faced an unusually deadly influenza virus. It sickened its first victims in the United States during the spring of 1918. Over the next year, the influenza killed more than 50 million people around the world. It was the deadliest pandemic in modern history.

In 1918, many cities set up temporary hospital camps to treat influenza patients.

Pandemic Similarities

The 1918 and COVID-19 pandemics were similar in several ways. Both were caused by highly contagious and unusually deadly viruses that

A mail carrier in New York wears a face mask while delivering mail. In 1918, many people wore masks while doing their jobs.

had never been seen in humans before. Both viruses also spread through respiratory droplets. When an infected person coughed, sneezed, or talked, people nearby could breathe in the droplets. The viruses could also survive on surfaces. So, a person could become infected by touching a contaminated surface and then touching the eyes, nose, or mouth.

Responses to the pandemics were also similar. In both 1918 and 2020, health departments encouraged basic hygiene practices to slow the spread of the viruses. These practices included washing hands to kill germs. People were also encouraged to remain socially distanced from others and to wear face masks in public. These measures helped stop people's respiratory droplets from spreading to others.

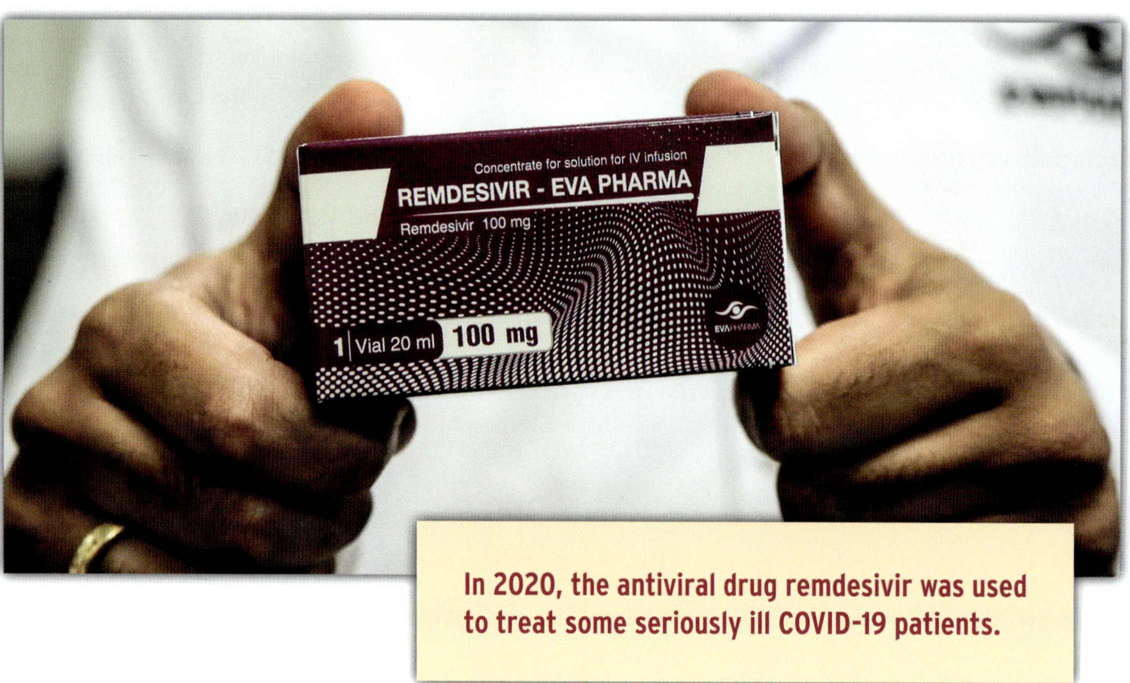

In 2020, the antiviral drug remdesivir was used to treat some seriously ill COVID-19 patients.

Differences

The world changed dramatically in the more than 100 years between the two pandemics. The population increased from about 1.8 billion people in 1918 to more than 7.5 billion in 2020. In 1918, viral science was brand new. Doctors were just beginning to understand the best ways to prevent and cure viral diseases. But by 2020, breakthroughs in science, medicine, and technology helped doctors better understand and treat viral diseases.

The 1918 pandemic helped shape the world's response to COVID-19. By 2020, hygiene practices popularized during the 1918 pandemic were commonplace. Health care also changed after the 1918 pandemic. Governments began treating health as a national concern rather than an individual's. This allowed many governments to coordinate federal responses to future pandemics.

Culture Shift

Both pandemics left an unmistakable impact on cultures around the world. Holiday celebrations, sporting events, and other large gatherings were discouraged or canceled for fear of spreading the viruses. People adopted new behaviors and health habits. Artists and entertainers expressed themselves in new and different ways as they tried to make sense of the pandemics. As movie theaters and museums closed their doors, the way audience members experienced this art and entertainment also shifted.

After the 1918 pandemic, some of these changes went away. But many remained permanent. Experts predicted that the COVID-19 pandemic would also cause permanent changes to society.

Elbow bumps became a popular alternative to handshakes during the COVID-19 pandemic.

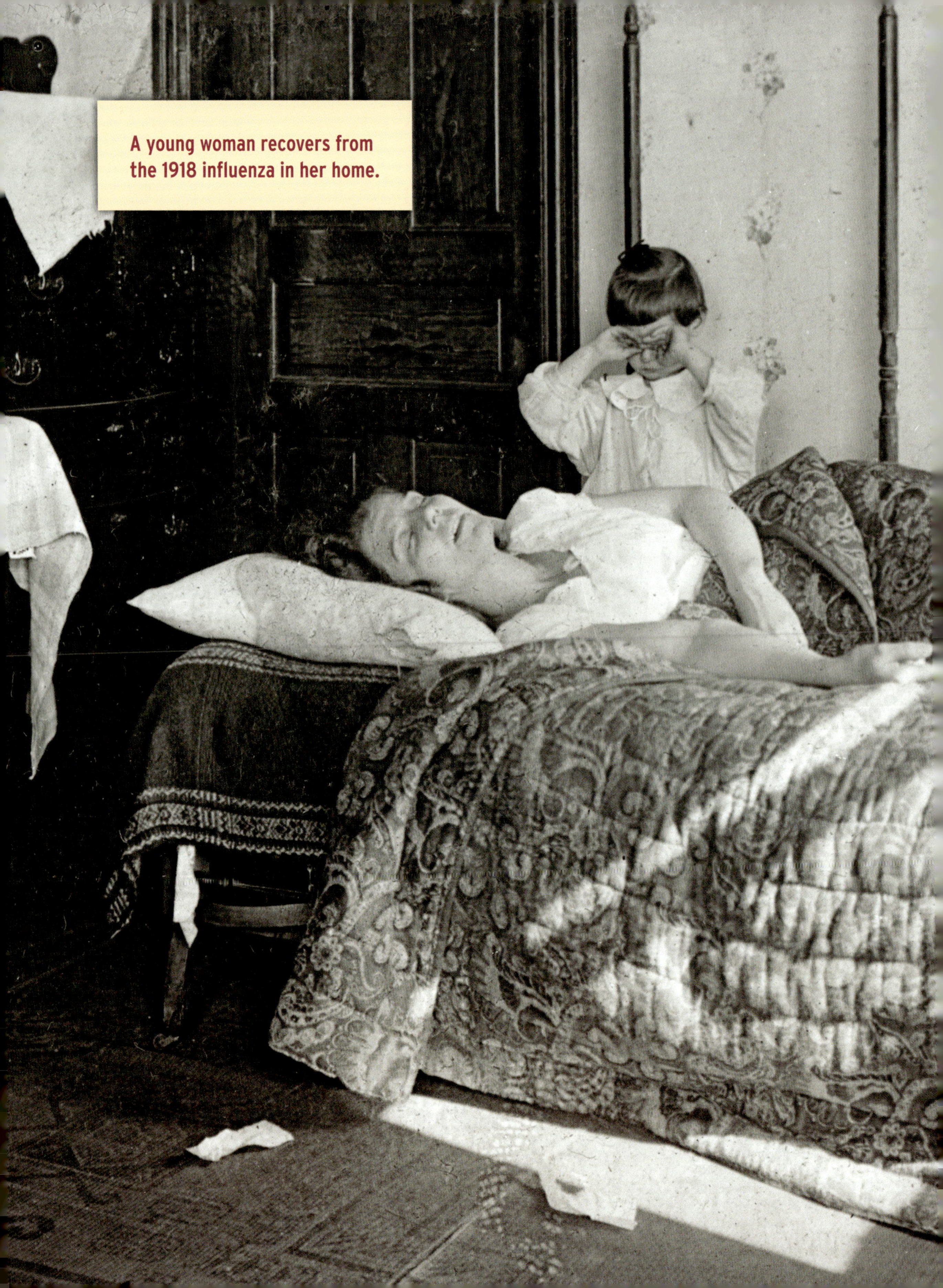

A young woman recovers from the 1918 influenza in her home.

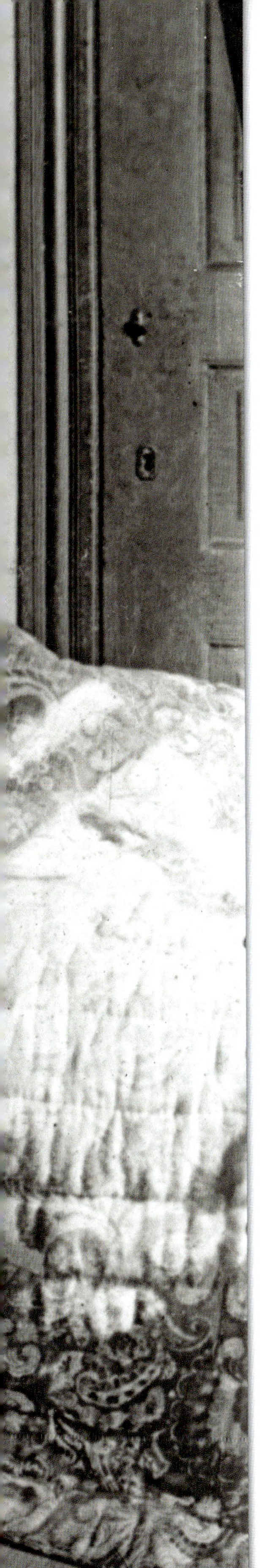

Chapter 2

INFLUENZA ATTACKS

Influenza, also called the flu, is a respiratory illness. Influenza viruses are common. Each year, the flu sickens millions of people in the United States alone, killing tens of thousands. Flu symptoms typically include fever, chills, stuffy or runny nose, muscle aches, cough, and fatigue. Most healthy people recover from the flu within two weeks.

But the 1918 influenza virus was different. It made people much sicker than a typical flu virus. It also killed more people. Flu viruses are usually deadliest in young children or elderly people. But the 1918 flu virus was also deadly for otherwise healthy adults aged 20 to 40.

Disease and War

The first recorded cases of the 1918 influenza were reported in March 1918 at Camp Funston, a US Army camp in Kansas. By the end of the month, the virus had sickened more than 1,000 of the camp's 54,000 soldiers, killing 38.

The flu wasn't the only problem facing the United States that year. World War I had started in 1914. During the war, the Allied forces of Great Britain, France, Russia, Romania, Italy, and Japan fought against the Central powers. These included Germany, Austria-Hungary, Bulgaria, and the Ottoman Empire. The United States had joined the war in 1917 on the side of the Allied forces.

In the spring of 1918, the US military sent more than 100,000 troops around the world to join the fighting. The troops carried the deadly virus with them. Influenza spread quickly on crowded military trains, ships, and battlefields. As much as 40 percent of the US Navy and 36 percent of the US Army contracted the flu.

World War I was triggered by the assassination of Archduke Franz Ferdinand of Austria-Hungary.

It didn't take long for the deadly virus to spread across Europe and Asia as well. Soldiers around the world became ill. In November 1918, World War I ended. But the pandemic was just beginning. Soldiers returning home brought the virus back with them.

Regular citizens were on the move as well. The war had forced many Europeans to leave their homelands to escape the fighting. These refugees traveled around the world. Many moved to big cities. There, crowded conditions helped the virus spread more quickly.

PANDEMICS BY THE NUMBERS

By the end of 1918, the influenza virus had killed about 45,000 US soldiers. Combat had killed 53,402 US soldiers.

US soldiers gargle with salt water. At the time, this was believed to prevent influenza infections.

Three Waves

Pandemics often occur in a series of waves. During each wave, infections increase dramatically before decreasing between the waves. The 1918 pandemic had three waves. The first began in spring. Some people infected during the first wave experienced severe symptoms, such as pneumonia. This infection causes the lungs to become inflamed. But most people experienced mild symptoms and recovered quickly.

Viruses can change as they spread from one person to another. This is called mutating. As the influenza virus spread in the spring, it mutated to become deadlier. In the fall of 1918, this mutated influenza caused the pandemic's second wave. This was the deadliest wave of the pandemic, killing hundreds of thousands of people in the United States alone. Most people died after contracting pneumonia.

Infections dropped by the end of 1918. However, they picked up for a third wave in January 1919. This third wave began in

Both King Alfonso XIII of Spain (*pictured*) and US president Woodrow Wilson became ill with influenza during the pandemic.

Australia and soon made its way back to the United States. By the summer of 1919, the pandemic had grown less severe. Those who recovered from the influenza became immune to the virus. With fewer people to infect, the virus eventually stopped circulating. By late 1919, the pandemic was over.

To this day, no one knows exactly how many people died from influenza during the 1918 pandemic. Death and illness reporting from the time is unreliable. However, some historians believe more than 500 million people were infected worldwide. This was one-third of the world's population. Historians also estimate that more than 50 million people died.

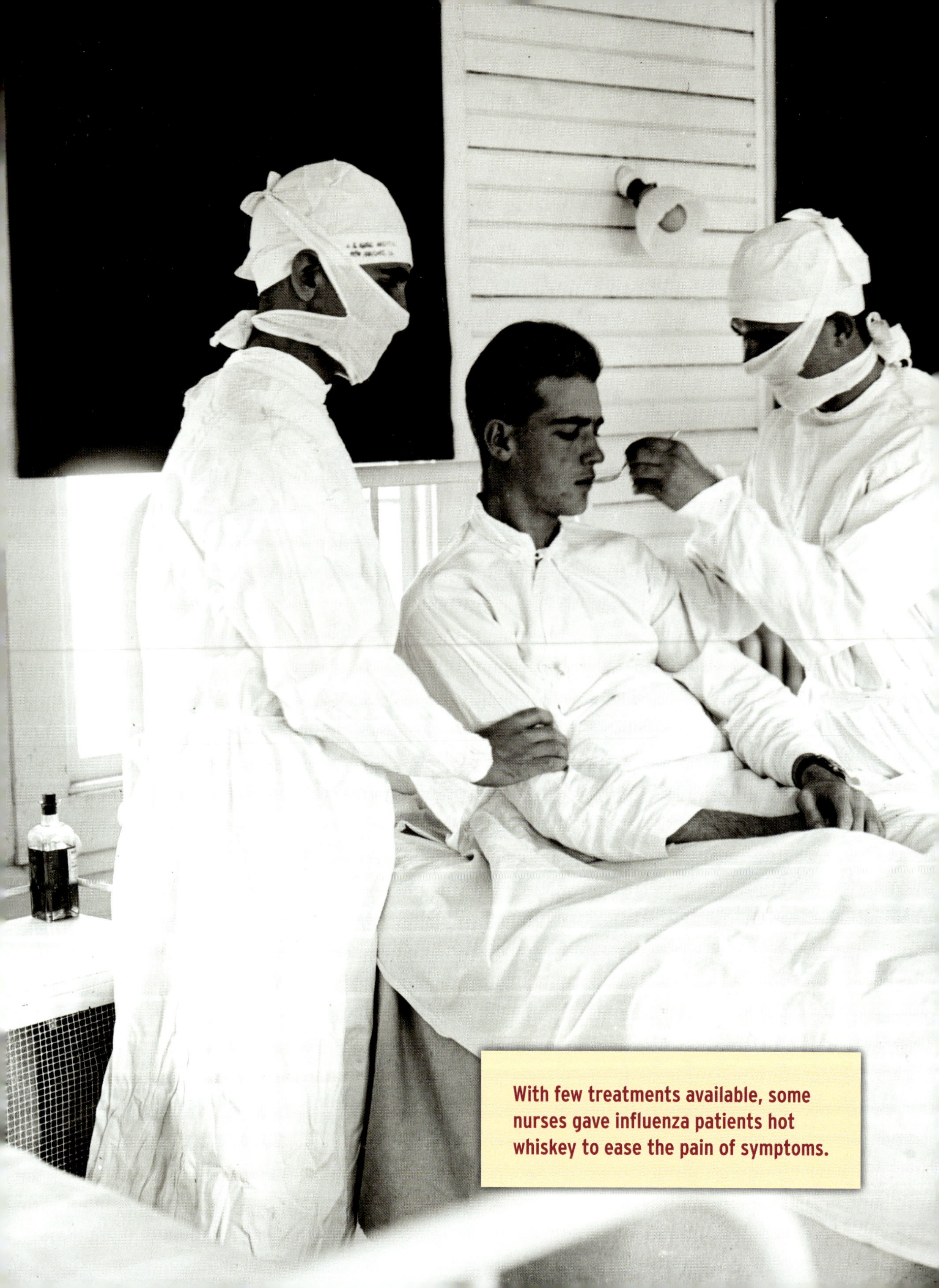

With few treatments available, some nurses gave influenza patients hot whiskey to ease the pain of symptoms.

Chapter 3

PANDEMIC CULTURE

The 1918 pandemic had a profound impact on culture. Over just a few years, it changed the way people behaved, worked, went to school, and socialized. It also triggered large-scale changes to society and art.

In the spring of 1918, health officials knew little about how to combat viruses. Scientists had long been able to study disease-causing germs called bacteria, using microscopes. Scientists knew that viruses were smaller than bacteria and that they caused some diseases. However, microscope technology was not yet advanced enough for scientists to observe and study viruses.

Given this lack of technology, scientists couldn't develop treatments for viral diseases, such as vaccines and antiviral medications. Instead, most health departments focused on preventing the spread of disease. Health officials could see that diseases like influenza spread more quickly in crowded and unclean conditions. So, they limited public gatherings

during the pandemic. And, they encouraged basic hygiene practices such as handwashing and sanitizing public places.

Masks Matter

Health officials also suspected that influenza was spread by droplets from the nose and throat. So, many US health officials encouraged medical professionals to wear face masks when treating influenza patients. Average citizens were also encouraged to wear face masks in public.

However, many people found masks uncomfortable and refused to wear them. Men often cut holes in their masks to smoke cigars through. Some women wore fashionable masks made of mesh called influenza veils. These did little to stop the virus.

Other hygiene practices were more accepted. Health officials found that germs didn't spread as quickly in ventilated areas. So, people were told to sleep with their bedroom windows open. In Minneapolis, Minnesota, streetcars were ordered to keep their windows open whenever carrying passengers. This rule was even enforced in the winter.

Some hygiene practices even became permanent. For example, health officials encouraged people to cover their mouths when coughing or sneezing. This was not a

In Seattle, Washington, people were not allowed to ride streetcars unless they were wearing face masks.

Many sports leagues continued despite the pandemic. Some players wore masks to protect themselves from influenza.

common practice before 1918. Cities also posted signs declaring it illegal to spit in public places. So, over time, it became less common for people to spit on the ground in public.

A Tale of Two Cities

Prevention measures helped slow the spread of influenza. However, these rules often varied by city, county, or state. Differing prevention measures meant the severity of influenza outbreaks varied greatly by community. Nowhere was this more apparent than in Philadelphia, Pennsylvania, and St. Louis, Missouri. These two cities took completely different approaches to the pandemic.

Philadelphia

In Philadelphia, city health officials downplayed the seriousness of the pandemic. The leader of the city's public health department believed the rise in flu deaths was caused by typical seasonal flu. As a result, city health officials implemented few health precautions. Schools, churches, and theaters remained open. On September 28, 1918, the city even held a huge parade. The parade drew more than

During World War I, Philadelphia held several large events to promote the war effort.

200,000 viewers, or one-ninth of Philadelphia's population. The city soon faced a surge in influenza cases. Within ten days, influenza had killed 1,000 people and sickened more than 20,000. City health officials quickly passed rules limiting gatherings and closing public places. However, these rules came too late to do much to stop the disease's spread.

St. Louis

St. Louis took a different approach than Philadelphia. Within days of the city's first flu case, city health officials closed schools, churches, and other public gathering places. They also ordered

Nurses in St. Louis helped transport flu patients to hospitals.

anyone who contracted the virus to quarantine at home. These measures kept the virus from spreading as quickly as in Philadelphia. From September to December 1918, St. Louis recorded 2,883 influenza deaths. Philadelphia recorded nearly 14,000 deaths. However, after its early success, St. Louis lifted its influenza prevention measures. A spike in cases and deaths soon followed.

Media Matters

Information about the pandemic, including how to prevent it, was primarily shared through print media. This included signs, newspapers, and magazines. Many newspapers were guilty of spreading incorrect information about the flu. During World War I, many countries controlled

When a disease affects a community, people in that community often try to blame it on outsiders. The 1918 influenza was often called the Spanish flu. In Spain, people blamed the influenza on the French. So, Spanish people called it the French flu.

During the COVID-19 pandemic, many people in Western countries blamed the virus on China, where it had originated. Because of this, people of Asian heritage in Western countries reported being the victims of racist words and attacks. Human rights organizations called on world leaders to stop anti-Asian abuse in their countries.

what information was released to the press. So, newspapers in warring countries focused on war updates instead of the flu. When newspapers did report on the flu, many downplayed its seriousness to keep public morale up. Warring countries also didn't want to reveal that their militaries were weakened by disease.

Since Spain was not involved in World War I, it was the first Western country to openly report on how deadly the influenza outbreak was. As a result, other countries falsely blamed the influenza on Spain. Many people referred to the disease as the Spanish flu. Historians still aren't sure where the virus originated.

Art and Literature

For many, the combination of the pandemic and World War I led to feelings of confusion and hopelessness. As a result, many artists embraced the Dada movement. This absurdist art style captured the uncertainty of the time.

Writers were also inspired by the sickness and death they saw around them. English author Virginia Woolf featured the influenza

Dada art often featured collages made of cut-up pieces of paper or magazines.

pandemic in her famous
book *Mrs. Dalloway*. The
book's title character,
Clarissa Dalloway, is a
pandemic survivor who
still suffers health issues.
British-American poet
T.S. Eliot penned his famous
poem "The Waste Land"
while recovering from
influenza. It reflects on how
bleak life seemed due to
the war and pandemic.

Virginia Woolf became seriously ill with influenza several times during the pandemic.

Spiritualism and Modernism

The combination of the war and the pandemic also created
a fascination with death. Spiritualism became popular. This
movement, originally popular during the mid-1800s, stemmed from
the idea that the living could communicate with the dead. During
the pandemic, people used séances, Ouija boards, and other
methods to try to talk to lost loved ones.

The pandemic also inspired a new architectural style called
modernism. It reflected the protection measures encouraged
during the pandemic. The style was airy, clean, and uncluttered.
Modernist buildings had large windows that improved ventilation.
They also featured smooth surfaces that could be easily cleaned.

In 1920, the Nineteenth Amendment to the US Constitution was adopted. It gave women the right to vote.

Chapter 4

A SOCIAL SHIFT

The social impacts of the 1918 pandemic can still be felt today. One impact was the rise of women in the US workforce. In 1918, American women were expected to stay home and care for their families. Men were more likely to work outside the home.

The flu was deadly for men between the ages of 20 and 40. World War I also killed many young adult men. The combined deaths of men during the war and the pandemic led to a shortage of male workers. Crops went unharvested. Trash, mail, and other public services were delayed. And, many businesses closed after too many employees fell ill.

With the sudden shortage of male workers, it became necessary and more socially acceptable for women to work outside the home. Women worked in factories, post offices, and in other places where men had traditionally worked. As more women entered the workforce, female workers organized to demand the same pay and rights as male workers. The fight for

equal rights would continue
for many years.

A New View on Health Care

The pandemic also shifted
attitudes on public health.
Previously, people in most
countries were responsible
for paying for medical
treatment themselves.
But health officials around
the world realized they
could better protect
citizens by providing
government-funded health

Some women worked as streetcar drivers during World War I. They were called conductorettes.

care. In the 1920s, many European countries began providing
national health-care subsidies to all citizens.

The United States did not implement national, subsidized health
care. But the country still made health a priority. In 1925, the United
States began requiring states to report disease data to the federal
government. This allowed the government to track where diseases
were spreading and develop strategies to fight them.

In 1946, the Communicable Disease Center was founded in
Atlanta, Georgia. The organization's original mission was to prevent
malaria, a disease spread by mosquitoes. However, it soon began
working to fight all contagious diseases. Today, the organization

A CDC scientist examines a machine used to spray insecticide.

is called the Centers for Disease Control and Prevention (CDC). Its scientists study how different diseases spread.

In 1948, diplomats from the United Nations launched the World Health Organization (WHO) to coordinate health care around the world. The WHO provides essential health services and medicines to those in need. It also advises governments on how to respond to health issues.

In 2017, WHO workers delivered medical supplies to the Democratic Republic of the Congo.

Science Breakthroughs

Science also moved forward after the 1918 pandemic. Electron microscopes were developed in the 1930s. These powerful tools allowed scientists to see and study viruses. As scientists learned more about viruses, they were able to develop vaccines and medicines to fight them.

The first influenza vaccine was approved for use in the 1940s. Scientists develop flu vaccines to target the strains of flu that are most likely to spread each year. A flu vaccine can reduce a person's chances of getting the flu by as much as 60 percent.

The first antiviral drugs were developed in the 1960s. People take antiviral drugs when they are already sick with influenza. Although antivirals don't cure the flu, they can help sick people recover more quickly.

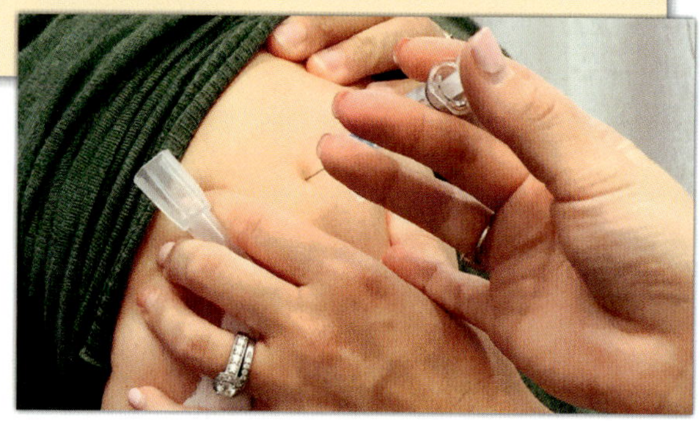

Today, the CDC recommends most Americans receive a flu vaccine each fall.

PANDEMICS BY THE NUMBERS

WORLDWIDE DEATHS CAUSED BY PANDEMICS FROM 1920–2019

1957–1958:
1.1 million deaths from influenza

1968:
1 million deaths from influenza

1981–2012:
36 million deaths from acquired immunodeficiency syndrome (AIDS)

A More Connected World

The world went through many other changes. International air travel became easier and more common. This helped diseases spread more quickly. The internet allowed people to communicate and access information faster than ever before.

As the world changed, it also experienced more pandemics. From 1957 to 1958, an influenza pandemic killed more than 1 million people. From 1981 to 2012, a disease called acquired immunodeficiency syndrome (AIDS) killed 36 million people.

These pandemics were not as deadly as the 1918 pandemic. However, health officials warned that the world was overdue for another large-scale disease outbreak. In 2019, their prediction came true.

World AIDS Day is commemorated every December to raise awareness about the disease.

Many nursing homes stopped allowing indoor visits during the pandemic. Instead, visits were held outdoors or through windows.

Chapter 5

COVID CULTURE

In late 2019, people in Wuhan, China, began getting sick with COVID-19. Scientists soon determined the disease outbreak was caused by a novel coronavirus, SARS-CoV-2. Coronaviruses cause upper respiratory infections in humans. The viruses are often responsible for common colds.

Health officials soon realized SARS-CoV-2 was different from a typical coronavirus. Some people with COVID-19 experienced mild, cold-like symptoms such as a cough and sore throat. Others experienced unusual symptoms, such as nausea and a loss of taste or smell. But for some, COVID-19 caused breathing problems, organ failure, and even death. People were at higher risk for complications if they had health conditions such as asthma. People 65 years old or older were also at higher risk. But even young, healthy individuals could be seriously affected by COVID-19.

In late 2019, COVID-19 spread from Wuhan to other parts of China. By early 2020, it had

spread to hundreds of countries around the world. On March 11, 2020, the WHO declared COVID-19 a pandemic. Leaders around the world struggled to contain a virus they still knew little about. As they did so, life changed for nearly everyone around the world.

A Piecemeal Approach

In the United States, President Donald Trump initially downplayed the seriousness of the pandemic. Although federal health experts provided recommendations to prevent COVID-19's spread, most public health decisions were left up to state governments.

States took different approaches to fighting COVID-19. Many issued stay-at-home orders in March and April. Under stay-at-home orders, people were asked to only leave their homes for necessary travel. Nonessential businesses had to close. These included movie theaters, salons, and shopping malls. Large gatherings were also prohibited. As the pandemic continued, some states issued mask mandates requiring people to wear face masks when out in public. However, some states never issued stay-at-home orders or mask mandates.

Many health experts believed this piecemeal approach was unsuccessful. In New Zealand, which had a strict national lockdown, only 0.04 percent of people had gotten COVID-19 by the end of 2020. Meanwhile, the United States had the most cases of any country in the world. By the end of 2020, about 6 percent of

In some states, people protested stay-at-home orders and mask mandates. They felt the rules violated their freedoms.

Americans had been infected. And, the United States was regularly recording more than 200,000 new COVID-19 cases each day.

Economic Crisis

As businesses closed under stay-at-home orders, Americans' shopping habits changed. Many people stocked up on toilet paper and other hygiene products at grocery stores. This created shortages that persisted for months.

As stores closed, many businesses struggled to make money and pay their employees. So, many businesses had to lay people off. By the end of April, 20.5 million Americans had lost their jobs.

Many Americans stocked up on food during the pandemic. This led to empty shelves at stores across the country.

By September, an estimated 100,000 US businesses had closed permanently. The government provided some financial aid to businesses and citizens. On March 27, US president Donald Trump had signed the Coronavirus Aid, Relief, and Economic Security (CARES) Act. This provided $1.8 trillion in aid to individuals and businesses, including direct payments of $1,200 to many Americans. However, many people still struggled to find work and pay bills.

Working from Home

Many types of businesses could allow employees to work from home. This prevented COVID-19 from spreading in office spaces. Some workers reported lower stress while working from home. However, other workers found it harder to focus.

Working from home could be especially stressful for parents. In March and April, many schools and day cares closed to prevent COVID-19's spread. As a result, many parents chose to reduce their hours or leave their jobs to care for their children. Women were especially affected by this choice. Eight times as many women as men chose to leave their jobs in 2020.

Learning Challenges

Although many schools were closed in spring 2020, students still needed to continue learning. So, many schools had students attend class virtually from home. This was called distance learning.

Teachers worked hard to make distance learning as effective as in-person education. But they faced challenges. Students with disabilities and those learning to speak English often struggled without in-person support. And, not all students had computers or reliable internet access. This was especially true for students of color, those in rural areas, and those from low-income families. Some school districts provided students with laptops and access to Wi-Fi. However, not all districts could afford to do so.

A new school year began in fall 2020. Some schools resumed full-time, in-person learning. Others continued distance learning. And, some schools tried a combination of both. At these schools, students took turns attending in-person class and virtual class. This meant fewer students attended class in person at one time. However, as COVID-19 cases increased in the United States during the late fall, many schools switched back to distance learning only.

Many teachers taught class virtually from their classrooms at school.

School custodians made sure that school buildings were kept sanitized and safe for in-person learning.

Staying Apart

In addition to missing out on learning opportunities, students missed socializing with their friends in person. Beginning in spring 2020, social gatherings were discouraged for children and adults alike. Proms, graduations, weddings, funerals, and other major social events were canceled or held with minimal attendees to avoid spreading COVID-19.

As the 2020 holiday season approached, people were also forced to rethink their celebrations. The virus could spread easily at crowded indoor gatherings. So, health experts discouraged celebrating with anyone outside of one's

Instead of holding a traditional graduation ceremony, one Florida school held a graduation car parade.

household. Many people were saddened that they could not see their friends and family members in person. However, people found ways to connect with loved ones virtually by using video chat apps. Others celebrated outdoors, which limited the virus's spread.

Sports and Entertainment

The pandemic also caused many professional sports leagues to cancel, postpone, or adapt their seasons. The National Basketball Association (NBA) suspended its season in March. The season restarted in July. However, fans were not allowed to attend the games. Major League Baseball (MLB) also held a shortened season with no fans in attendance.

As movie theaters closed under stay-at-home orders, interest in streaming services surged. During the pandemic, more than

Some baseball teams displayed cardboard cutouts of fans in the stands during games.

12 million people joined streaming services, such as Hulu, Disney+, or Netflix. Some new movies, such as Disney's live-action *Mulan*, were released exclusively on streaming services. Other movies, including the new *Black Widow* film, had their releases delayed.

Musicians also adapted to life during the pandemic. With in-person concerts canceled, some artists held virtual concerts over social media. Other artists used their time at home to record new music, which they released via music-streaming services such as Spotify.

Depressed and Divided

As the pandemic wore on, people reported increasing levels of

In July 2020, singer-songwriter Taylor Swift stunned fans when she announced she would release a surprise new album on music-streaming services. Swift had to cancel her planned summer concert tour because of COVID-19. So, instead of touring, she wrote and recorded a new album in just a few months! Swift's album, *Folklore*, included the song "Epiphany," which was written about health-care workers battling COVID-19. The album was praised by critics and fans alike.

Before *Folklore*, Swift released the album *Lover* in August 2019.

anxiety and depression. The lack of in-person socializing left many people feeling lonely and isolated. In June 2020, about 24 percent of adult Americans reported symptoms of depression. This was four times the rate reported during the same period in 2019. To make matters worse, the country seemed more politically divided than it had been in decades.

In the United States, 2020 was the year of a presidential election. Former Democratic vice president Joe Biden ran against President Trump for the US presidency. People's political opinions influenced how they behaved during the pandemic. For example, President Trump's supporters were less likely to wear face masks. Biden's supporters were more likely to follow health guidelines. They were also more likely to support closing nonessential businesses.

Trump (*left*) and Biden practiced social distancing during the first presidential debate.

The two presidential candidates campaigned very differently. Trump held large, in-person rallies and sent supporters to knock on doors. Biden held smaller, socially distanced rallies and virtual gatherings. In a close election in November, Americans elected Joe Biden the next president of the United States.

An Unknown Future

As 2021 began, the pandemic was far from over. In January, the world surpassed 100 million COVID-19 cases. More than 2 million people had died. But the news wasn't all bad.

Since the start of the pandemic, scientists had been working to develop a COVID-19 vaccine. In December 2020, COVID-19 vaccines from drug companies Pfizer and Moderna were approved for emergency use in the United States. Health-care workers and other high-risk individuals were among the first to be vaccinated. It would take time to produce and distribute the vaccines. But health experts believed most adult Americans would be vaccinated by summer 2021.

Even with an end in sight, many wondered whether some changes caused by the COVID-19 pandemic would be permanent. For example, experts predicted Americans would wear face masks during future cold and flu seasons. Although no one knew for sure how COVID-19 would affect US culture, Americans were hopeful the pandemic would change their nation for the better.

TIMELINE

1914
World War I begins.

MARCH 1918
The first cases of pandemic influenza are reported at Camp Funston in Kansas. That spring, troop movements help the disease spread worldwide.

1919
The 1918 influenza pandemic comes to an end.

1917
The United States joins World War I on the side of the Allied forces.

FALL 1918
The second and deadliest wave of influenza strikes.

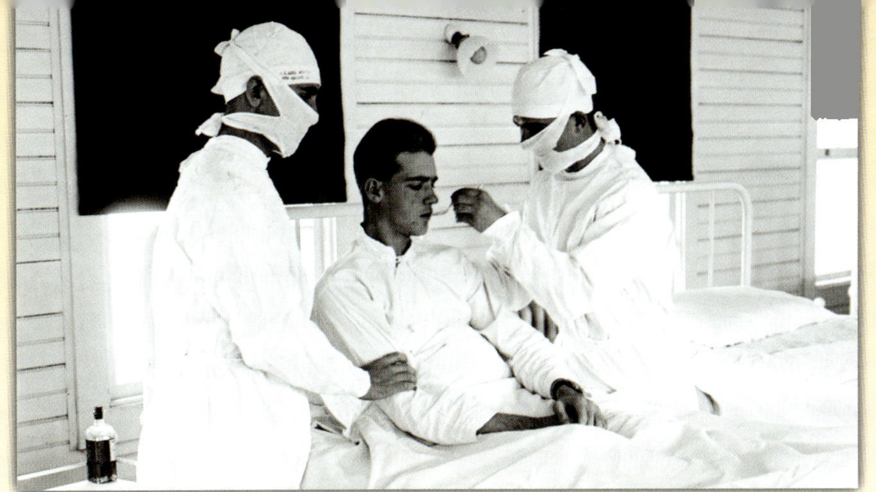

1946

The Communicable Disease Center is founded in Atlanta, Georgia. It later becomes the Centers for Disease Control and Prevention (CDC).

1948

The United Nations founds the World Health Organization (WHO).

DECEMBER 2019

A new disease is discovered in Wuhan, China. It is later named COVID-19.

JANUARY 2021

More than 100 million COVID-19 cases have been reported worldwide, and more than 2 million people have died.

MARCH 11, 2020

The WHO declares COVID-19 a pandemic.

NOVEMBER 2020

Joe Biden is elected president of the United States.

LATE APRIL 2020

More than 20 million Americans have lost their jobs because of the COVID-19 pandemic.

DECEMBER 2020

COVID-19 vaccines from drug companies Pfizer and Moderna are approved for emergency use in the United States.

GLOSSARY

absurdist—of or relating to the belief that humans exist in an irrational, chaotic universe.

Centers for Disease Control and Prevention (CDC)—the main national health organization in the United States. The CDC works to control the spread of disease and maintain and improve public health in the United States and other countries.

depression—a state of feeling sad or dejected.

disability—a condition that interferes with a person's physical or mental abilities.

droplet—a tiny drop of liquid.

hygiene—conditions or practices of cleanliness that are required for good health.

immune—incapable of being affected by a disease. Immunodeficiency is a condition in which the body cannot produce enough cells to fight infection.

mandate—an official order.

media—a form or system of communication, information, or entertainment. It includes television, radio, and newspapers.

novel—new and different from what has previously been known.

Ouija board—a board with an alphabet and other symbols used to seek messages from spirits.

outbreak—a sudden increase in the occurrence of illness.

quarantine—to separate from others in order to stop a disease from spreading.

racist—having the belief that one race is better than another.

refugee—a person who flees to another country for safety and protection.

respiratory–having to do with the system of organs involved with breathing.

sanitize–to make something free from disease by cleaning it.

séance–a meeting held by a spiritualist to communicate with spirits.

shortage–a lack of something that is needed.

socialize–to talk and do things with other people.

subsidy–a government grant to a person or a company. Something that has a subsidy is subsidized.

United Nations–a group of nations formed in 1945. Its goals are peace, human rights, security, and social and economic development.

ventilation–the process of allowing fresh air to enter and move through. An area with good ventilation is ventilated.

World Health Organization (WHO)–an agency of the United Nations that works to maintain and improve the health of people around the world.

Booklinks
NONFICTION NETWORK
FREE! ONLINE NONFICTION RESOURCES

To learn more about pandemic culture shifts, please visit **abdobooklinks.com** or scan this QR code. These links are routinely monitored and updated to provide the most current information available.

INDEX

A

acquired immunodeficiency syndrome (AIDS), 30–31
antiviral drugs, 17, 30
Army, US, 11–12
Australia, 14–15

B

Biden, Joe, 42–43

C

Camp Funston, 11–12
Centers for Disease Control and Prevention (CDC), 28–29
China, 5, 23, 33
closures, 9, 22, 27, 35–37, 40, 42
Coronavirus Aid, Relief, and Economic Security (CARES) Act, 37
COVID-19
    cases, 5, 35–36, 38, 43
    deaths, 5–6, 43
    spread, 5, 7, 9, 33–34, 37, 39–40
    symptoms, 33

D

Dada movement, 24
depression, 41–42

E

Eliot, T.S., 25

F

face masks, 7, 18–19, 35, 42–43

H

health care, 8, 28–29
holidays, 9, 39–40
hygiene practices, 7–8, 18–19, 36

I

influenza (1918)
    cases, 11, 15, 22–23
    deaths, 6, 12, 14–15, 21–23, 27
    mutation, 14
    spread, 6–7, 9, 12–15, 17–20, 22–23
    symptoms, 11, 14

L

large gatherings, 9, 17, 22, 35, 39–40, 43
lockdowns, 34–36, 40

M

Moderna, 43
modernism, 25
movie theaters, 9, 21, 35, 40

N

Navy, US, 12
New Zealand, 35
1957 influenza pandemic, 30–31
1968 influenza pandemic, 30

P

Pfizer, 43
Philadelphia, Pennsylvania, 21–23
pneumonia, 14
print media, 23–24

R

racism, 23

S

schools, 17, 21–22, 37–39
seasonal influenza, 11, 21, 43
shopping, 36
social distancing, 7, 43
socializing, 5, 17, 39–40, 42
Spanish flu, 23–24
spiritualism, 25
sporting events, 9, 40
St. Louis, Missouri, 21–23
stay-at-home orders, 34–36, 40
streaming services, 40–41
Swift, Taylor, 41

T

Trump, Donald, 34, 37, 42–43
2020 presidential election, 42–43

U

unemployment, 36–37
United Nations, 29

V

vaccines, 17, 30, 43
viral science, 8, 17, 28–30, 33, 43

W

women's rights, 27–28
Woolf, Virginia, 24–25
working from home, 37
World Health Organization (WHO), 29, 34
World War I, 12–13, 23–25, 27